PLASTIC SURGERY 2040

By Tim Dominguez

Chapter 1

Happy couple

2025, advancement in robotics and codes for face symmetry helps in plastic surgery as certain parts are constructed and perfectly attached to humans along with the removal of melanoma and other skin growths. 2027, robotics perform simple surgeries. 2030, The first non surgeon assisted cosmetic facial attachment completed. 2033, plastic surgery is done on other parts of human anatomy with no surgeon assisting. 2040, A Los Angeles enhancement facility opens and has the only 25 story non-surgeon cosmetic office in the world that does entire body, plastic and reconstructive surgeries. It took 15 years for the surgical coding practitioner to create this office into a 5 billion dollar a year business. Procedures such as nose jobs, facelifts and breast implants take a day no matter the complications. The system can create anything in a 3D image and the coding finds a way to attach it to the human body.

They are also experimenting with organ and heart valve replacement and just did an 80 year old man for the first time, switching all 4 valves with printed new ones and keeping the old ones for analysis. Doing that and having the human genome and a person's DNA, now are experimenting with 3D printing human limbs instead of trying to grow them like other facilities attempted to do.

How this all works is a woman wants a nose job and picks from one of the 3d images of what her idea is of the perfect nose, then it's uploaded and within 5 minutes the procedure is started. A 3D skin tissue print is created and brought by conveyor belt to the patient then robotic surgical tools do the rest. A woman goes through the front door as a brunette, hair thinning, facial deformities, any problem with any part of the body. Then the same day comes out the back door becoming a redhead, a brunette, braided, with perfect facial and body features.The office can even change their skin pigment from pale white to dark golden brown or black and do the opposite as well. Sometimes caucasian women only want to be black with a different nose and cheeks for 3 or 4 months then switch back. Or a black woman wants to be Asian for a few months, have eyes and lips and nose done, then have another surgery to be back to her original self.

Founder Doug Simpson who's been married to Kim since high school and grew together to create 2 kids and the surgical complex. They are one big happy family with Kim being a stay at home mom and Doug working 14 hour days and is also very happy sexually because his office assistant is keeping him that way. The kids are 5 and 7 in the best schools. A great facade to the outside world and treated like royalty in L.A. They appear on talk shows, and always get tables at impossible restaurants. At night he comes home kissing the kids and his wife who is allowed $20,000.00 a month for shopping and always has different lingerie for every evening of the week. She's trying to get her husband to notice her but sex only happens four times tops every few weeks with looks of disinterest but she keeps trying. He would rather be with the assistant who is a proper knee high skirts, button up blouse next door type, but in the bedroom is waiting with legs open and 3 inch high heels on top of the bed. She knows he likes it real hot and dirty and she likes making it that way.

Their house is also getting remodeled right now, so it's very busy around the family. They try to help the less fortunate and believe everyone deserves a second chance so they hire a company that has ex-cons employed to redo the kitchen and patio next to the pool. They are coming and going out of the house while all this is going on. Some even flirt and Kim likes it but doesn't follow through being happily married and all, but in the back of her mind if she ever decided to she thinks it would be fun.

With the wife hardly visiting the office anymore it's a big surprise when she shows up. Kim wanted to show her naughty side and came up to the office on a Friday with a long coat and nothing underneath during lunch. He was with a picky patient who couldn't decide on the perfect chin and after the guard lets her in, she makes her way through his assistants and sits at his desk. Opening and closing drawers while she is waiting, seeing what's lying around his computer. She notices her wedding photo on the corner of the desk, a photo of the kids, then sees a small heart drawn on a note along with a phone call message. Kim knows who writes down the messages and it was a normal note about calling somebody back. But why draw the heart? The assistant wasn't there so she stepped out to that person's desk to peak around a little bit. A post note poking out from underneath the laptop reads, "go out to lunch and buy those fuck me pumps for this afternoon oxoxox" in her husbands writing. "That mother fucker"! She said to herself "I have been trying to get a lot more sex from him and he's getting all he wants from work." Hearing the elevator door open she runs back to Dougs office as Debbie goes to her desk with a shoe bag. Walking back out saying hi to her, " I noticed the bag, had a good lunch?" " Yes I did, shopping on lunch always makes a girls day better." Kim - "Yes it does, what did you buy?" "Some shoes?" Kim- "can I see?" "Ok they are for clubbing." Kim -'You must like getting crazy at the clubs?" "Yep." Doug shows up a couple of minutes later and is very surprised to see his wife there and tells Kim that Debbie is going to get some cosmetic surgery done very soon.

After all three talked for a few minutes Doug and Kim walk back into the office, she shuts the blinds and gets on her knees and unzips his fly. She's trying but he's not getting hard but keeps at it anyway. The not so fun session ends and when he goes into the bathroom to clean up she gets the chair and moves it to the corner and stands on it to shift the security camera, aiming it right at his desk then steps down and moves the chair back in the nick of time. She grabs his phone because she knows it has all the security cameras linked to it and will just say she grabbed his by mistake since they have the same phone. Walking away she turns and sees him leaning over Debbies shoulder and discussing something.

CHAPTER 2

Betrayal

Kim puts the dinner in the oven that evening, Doug and Debbie are having an hour of sex in his office. She is looking at his phone and taking in the conversation, Debbie- "You're going to make me perfect honey? perfect breasts, perfect face, perfect butt?" "Yes, I have a special code for you when you go under the knife that will make you better than all the others." "all the areas you think are flaws will be gone." Your b cups will now be double DD's and your nose will be perfect." "After you are done with perfecting me you're going to get rid of that bitch?" Doug: "Yes It will happen next week my love." After the sex the lovers look at the 3d images of what she wants on her body. Kim is pissed as the lovers are enjoying picking, reshaping and adding to her look on the computer. They are also talking about moving all the money over and the kids in boarding schools after the wife is taken care of. Debbie kisses and tells Doug "I am going to be your perfect wife." "Have our own kids." Doug "Yes, my wife is a bad mom, spoiling them to no end and lousy in bed and she is so fucking boring." "It will all be taken care of in a few days." " Also now we have the Island in the caribbean I purchased. Totally undeveloped to do what we want with. I sent out the word to everyone on nearby islands to stay out of our waters so no one goes near our paradise. Debbie " Oh shit, our very own island." Doug " Oh yes, It's all ours, we will develop it into the ultimate private party island. Create you your own palace.'

Kim is seething and scared and just learning about this damn island he bought under her nose. She checks it out more while they are still busy. After they finally leave the office and Doug comes home about 8:30 pm, Kim puts some sleeping pills mixed in his food so he doesn't wake up and decides to sneak out and go to the office. Dismissing all of the cleaning crew and security, she now goes up to the surgical area and the 3d build section and with the desktop starts opening files. Gets to Debbies and looks through images saying to herself "I'm going to fuck up her face." Then sees what alterations are being done to her body as well and knows how to upload for surgery because when the office was small she would do it all for him. All the time thinking, how many other woman has he fucked

In the meantime Debbie is at home thinking about the parties, the world travels they will be taking, she has a publicist picked out, has names lined up for the kids she will be having. Buying bigger bras for her soon to be DD boobs. She has maintained the relationship as a secret, but the big reveal will be in a couple of months after the chaos following the disappearance of his wife dies down. She grew up very poor, had to go to a smaller college then move up to a bigger one, never having new clothes, always 2nd hand stuff so feels she is owed it right fuckin now. She does think about what if he's caught. But then the other side of the coin is what if he isn't caught and they get away with being such a power couple in L.A. She's insecure but very skanky in bed. She has another man on the side for the type of sex she likes and is not sure she will end it when they are totally together. She promised all her friends plastic surgery discounts when she becomes the Mrs. but the clock is ticking as her last hours of being normal are coming to an end.

With Kim now going through tons of images she stumbled across dogs and the idea came into her head. Puts in an internet search for dirty mongrels. Finds full body and face images and scans and has them turned into actual 3d parts. The multimillion dollar printers at the facility have samples of everything from dogs to apes to humans and can replicate millions of hairs, tissue and bone in minutes because another section of offices deals with tissue and hair repair for animals at zoos. For the next 2 hours the printers are getting everything ready for human placement. Creating hair and bone additions and placing finished prepped units on conveyor belts to the remote arms next to the surgery table. While this is happening she is erasing all of Debbie's entire files from the facility and has some really dark plans she is going to act out. She also has full knowledge of meds for making someone go numb or sleep. About 11:00 pm she texts Debbie saying he has everything ready and just comes now so it's done tonight and let's just get it over with.

Chapter 3

Scalpels

She drives up to the facility and gets there about 11:30 p.m. and the parking lot is totally empty but the lights are all on. Kim puts on a mask so you can't see her face and texts her that he is getting the machines ready and to go up to room 205. When she gets there to undress and wash up and lay naked on the table and to leave her phone there and write down her password so he can take before and after pics, I am busy finishing the details. Debbie cleans up and comes into the room like he told her too and there are placements to put her hands in because she wanted permanent long nails. There are finger holders with straps over the knuckle to each finger to keep them still and also wrist straps to keep her hands from moving.

Stirrups because she wants her legs worked on with having her hair permanently removed which also has straps to go on her ankles and knees and thighs and also one for her neck. She manages to work her limbs into all the loose loops then looks around and notices that the conveyor belts have stuff on them but they are covered by towels. After she is set on the table Kim presses a button and all the straps tighten at the same time. Then with a tension dial gives it a turn to make her straps even tighter so she is absolutely at the wifes mercy. A robotic arm comes out, one of 30 arms in the surgery room injecting her neck with a numbing concoction. Debbie hears footsteps coming, she is happy because she thinks it's her lover but Kim walks out and stands over the table right in her face, pulls her mask down and says, " hi you fuckin bitch." "You're going to destroy my family, well that's not going to happen." "Since you were such a dirty disgusting bitch for being with a married man. My married man! I thought you should look on the outside what you are on the inside." "Look at the screen, your going to be changed to that fuckin 4 legged ugly mongrel. Right now your body is numb, you can't move but you can talk which will be taken care of first." She anchors down the strap on Debbies neck, "A robotic arm will go down your throat cutting vocal cords and then fuse them back together to sound like a tiny poodle. I programmed the sound wave and it was put into code and the computer calculated the alterations needed to be done to them to give you the sound of a weeping puppy. You wanted a voice alteration to be more sultry but I thought this would fit you better."

Debbie- " Oh fuck, sorry, I will leave your family alone, please god please no." Screaming " stop!" " Fucking stop!" "Fucking please stop!' "God damn it, you must stop!"

Kim- " Wow, the empty offices sound so cool, I didn't realize when you scream you can hear an echo." " Here comes the arm with the cutting tools, I am just going to sit back and enjoy the show." She kisses Debbie on the forehead and it freaked her out because she felt it and knows she is going to feel extreme pain soon. "When you are finished, I have a cousin that lives in the Louisiana bayou, he knows the shit you pulled on me and is excited you're going to be his new pet." "Oh yea, I'm going to leave you fertile so you can have his children. She then holds up Debbie's drivers license, credit cards, and birth certificate. I am going to take a trip pretending to be you and I will make it look like you drowned, then cut up all of your personal info and sell all your shit. You don't exist anymore. Look up, I put that mirror up there so you can see all the work being done to you. Then the last thing that is programmed is to burn your corneas so your mongrel face is that last thing you ever see in this world.

Then removes the towels so Debbie can see her jagged dog teeth that won't allow her mouth to shut. She selected them from different canines, 7 extra inches of tongue so it's always hanging out and large extra nose bone as well as the other additions." As she screams, the arm extends and works its way down her throat as she is gagging, Kim listens excitedly as her voice is cutting in and out and hearing the blades giving off a deep buzzing sound coming out of Debbies mouth while partially choking on the instrument.

Kim ``You're going to feel every single dog hair that will be inserted into your body. All your human hair will be shaved off and every follicle inserted will feel like giant stinging needles going into your body. The prepping has been going on for hours, making dog teeth, nipples, whiskers, and especially the bone structure for your new giant snout. The cleaning crew is gone for the night, I used my husband's email to send everyone away, it's just you and me. I uploaded the entire anatomy of a dog, which took quite a while for the gcode to slice up and figure out how to convert from human anatomy. Your tendons, muscles and skin in your elbows and knees will be cut, pulled and restitched so your limb movements match that mongrel perfectly. Kim then laughs as she walks away letting the robotic arms do their dirty work.

From the screaming her voice starts turning into a gurgly bark when the arm that was in her throat slowly comes out. It stops where her molars once were and cuts the muscles in her jaw so it stays open for what comes next.

A Raspy bark starts coming out of her mouth and constant dog whines from the pain as each hair is pulled off her body one by one and given a light electro shock so it wont grow back. After all the hair is removed 15 robotic arms move out over her body and face.

The electric motors have a low whiney noise to them as they get into position. 9 of them hovering over her body all have scalpels. The 5 over her face are to pulverize her facial bones for realignment. One over her nose, 2 on each side of her cheek bones and 2 on each side of her jaw. The tools are similar to the ones that go on top of a cow, hitting them on the head to kill them but in miniature form. A small piston will be forced down by a hydraulic motor to do precise busting punches to her bone structure destroying that area with pin point accuracy.The 10th robotic arm has pinchers and moves up to her head while her mouth is kept open and starts pulling her teeth out, It was programmed to take 20 seconds of slow pulling for each tooth and then when it was done grabs her tongue tight. a suction tube comes in and sucks the blood from around her mouth and gauzes the sides of her face. Those tools all are now retracted and away from her so the real show can begin. All is dead quiet for about 30 seconds. Then at the same time the 5 bone breaking tools go off, a loud pop and her nose is smashed in. Both sides of her jaw shatter, her cheek bones cave in, Then the pistons move an inch and repeat, breaking more of her face up. They retract up and now 3 scalpels come in and cut thru her skin from under her chin going up to the ridge of her nose and all 3 keep going in circular motion 4 times going back around her chin and over her nose again going all the way through. 4 Pistons move next to her rib cage as her face is still being worked on. A robotic arm grabs the long piece of 3d printed dog tongue off the conveyor belt and the tip of hers is sliced off and now it's being attached. The pincers move all the way to the end of her new tongue about 10 inches from her face and pulls it down so it's out of the way for the next step.

Kim was turned on while watching behind glass in a side office with her panties totally soaked. She had to start fingering herself and came several times, especially when Debbie's jaw was being altered. She loved seeing the teeth being pulled out slowly as her body tightened up right before each one got their final hard tug to come out. Kim at this point has one hand pulling on her nipple hard as the other is going as fast as she can get it to move between her legs. She wants to see that island that he wants no one to come around to. Kim wants more so after cumming hard for the 4th time just sits there relaxed as the best torture is about to come.

A tool extends into her mouth with 4 spikes on it, as soon as its most of the way in, right before getting to where her face is cut it protrudes 2 into the roof of her mouth going through her cheeks sticking out of her face and the 2 on both sides of her tongue going through the bottom of her mouth out of her jaw. Now the 4 slowly pull her jaw and nose forward and the whole front of her face is leaving the rest of her head. 2 other arms are grabbing the large long bones to put in the gap for her snout as well as the gums to hold the jagged teeth . 6 inches of bones are being fused with the front part of chin and jaw and the back new reinforced jaw socket being built to handle the extra weight and structure. She has blacked out a few times but Kim keeps giving her small Electro shocks to her heart to keep her waking up. A constant low painful noise comes from the back of her throat. Her face is red and swollen from such trauma but it keeps going. Extra muscle and nerves and skin being attached over the new bone. Now pushing whiskers into her nose while a scalpel cuts the tops of her ears off and attaching long folded over dog ears. She is screaming for death begging over and over to die.

Scalpels cut her entire breasts off and her skin sewn back up with 8 nipples now being attached. 2 scalpels cut each side of her, a rectangular shape so skin can be pulled and expose her rib cages. 2 Pistons start hammering both sides at the same time cracking ribs with 2 lower ones being removed to give her a narrow lower half of her body. After ribs are broken they are pushed in to give her a more narrow look and fused back together, making her have a very hard time to breath now that it's constricting her lungs. She has to breathe through her mouth now with the cold air being sucked in hurting all her cuts and open wounds in her mouth.

Two arms come out on each side of the table next to her hands and feet. Lasers come on and starts slicing through each finger and toe down to knuckle then another laser blackens and coderizes what's left to make the dog paws. After the paws were done, The stirrups moved up and towards her so her legs are in a sitting position.

Scalpels slice across the acls and mcls and the muscles are cut and stitched tighter together so she can no longer straighten her legs. Tears are in a constant stream and her eyes are bugging out from pain. Her arms are cut into and the same things are happening. The muscles and skin and tendons are being trimmed and reattached so she can barely bend her elbows anymore except for maybe absorbing the shock from jumping down off a bed or couch. Now that her torso is sewn up the pistons move to her hips and bust her hip bones and they are fused to limit stretching movement without feeling severe pulling and pain.

But Kim programmed it to take an inch more from one hip so she is kept off balance and has to walk with a strange limp for now on. Everything has finally stopped, she is swollen and bloody everywhere. Then she hears a motor start up and all of sudden, the room is moving on her. She is being rotated so she is facing the floor and there is a gap on the bed so spinal surgery can be Done. The scalpels start on her shoulder blades and move inward to the middle of her back and cut a long slit from the base of her neck through her back down to the beginning of her butt exposing her spinal cord. Then at the bottom moving outward to her hips creating flaps on both sides. Robotic arms open up the flaps having her entire insides exposed. A machine comes down and starts tweeking her vertebrae and she starts vomiting her dinner from last night. Vomiting and urinating over and over from the pain and shock, not able to control either anymore and got the runs a couple of times. The machines are pulling on her back to give her a hunch and at the same time removing her collar bones with 4 other mechanical arms.

CHAPTER 4

Dog Human

Everything retracts, a motor whine starts and she is rotated back around. Staring at the ceiling, barely able to see through her watery eyes, she sees her new horrible fate in the mirror and lays there for about 10 minutes just shaking her head slightly back and forth. Then one robotic arm appears over her eyes, the Laser fires into her cornea burning one and then the other and now her world is forever dark. It's 4 a.m., during this time Kim is coordinating moving the dog human beast to her cousins. She calls him up.

Kim-" She is done, laying across the table recovering.
I just sent you some pics."

Buck-" Wow, your revenge is absolute. I can't wait to show her who's boss

Kim- " I want you to treat her like shit. I want you to mistreat that bitch, make her feel it. Don't ever feel sorry for her because she was planning on killing me.

Buck-" What about your husband? He was planning on doing it too?"

Kim- " I decided to let it go with him , he still provides and is a good dad to the kids. "

She starts up Debbie's car and is able to maneuver her into it and tie her up. On the way out she stops and fills up then leaves a message for her husband telling him her cousin in Louisiana had an emergency and she needed to be there. Also texts her husband using Debbie's phone telling him she is through with him and found somebody with a bigger dick and good money and doesn't ever want to see him again. Stopping in empty fields along the way so she could be walked out and taken to the bathroom, She loves watching Debbie squat to take a dump and lift leg to pee and giving her soups and stuff she can suck down with a straw because she can't move her jaw yet. She sticks her long snout in water to slurp it up even though she can move her very long tongue that she has full control of. The human dog has on a heavy duty leash and a shock collar in case she tries to escape but has no fingerprints, no voice, she's just making sure and people should just think of her as a big fucking ugly dog. One time out in a field in texas she was squatting and a dog showed up and started smelling her ass. She tried to move out of the way so Kim pulled her by the collar to sit still and let the german shepherd smell her backside. The dog then tried to get on her back and mount her. Kim pulled her finally away from the dog but told her to get used to male dogs doing that because that's the only dick she's going to get. Midway through Texas she is thinking this is as good a place as any to get rid of the phone, she destroys Debbies phone so there is no longer a trace of her after resetting to original condition then tossing sim card one direction and sd card and battery in another. During the journey up to that point, she was texting all of Debbie's family and friends and posting on her social media that she is on a spur of the moment trip and was also taking pics along the way and sending them.

Her cousin has already started prepping things, making a dog house and other surprises. Cousin Buck is single, loves the swamp but is so far out women are hard to find who aren't already married. Even though Buck graduated he hated school and does manual labor at the local warehouse for a living. At 38 he thinks he still will meet someone but is ready to be a father. He adores his cousin and even though this is just so bizarre and sinister it sounds like a fool proof opportunity. Plus sexually he has a bit of weirdness to him anyway.

Now arriving, unties her and walks her out of the car and Debbie see's what she is in for. 4 large mastiffs, all males and a pink dog house, also a bar next to that with shackles. Kim asks where can we dump her car after tying her collar to the cyclone fence he built around the small enclosure. There's barely enough room for the mastiffs and her to move around in. Buck tells her Debbie is going to stay in that area and the mastiffs have full run of the yard and at night in the house. For right now he wants to protect her for his own child bearing reasons. They drive for a while with Kim following behind and are going far into the bayou. Buck opens all the windows and drives the car into the swamp where he knows it's deep, sinking slowly into the thick mud. Kim turns to him and says "now take care of that bitch" and flies back to California. On the plane, Buck is sending pics of what's going on with his new pet and she is texting her husband talking about the family and how she was against him having plastic surgery but now has decided to be in favor of it. Then texts her parents asking if they can watch the kids next week .

Kim is motivated and starts sexting 2 of the parolees doing the remodel and by the time the flight ended she had gone inside the plane's bathroom and sent both naughty pics and they sent her some back. They plan on a secret meeting for the next evening. She flirts with them and tells them she is turned on by both and can't choose. Kim throws out the silly question, what if you both can have your way with me. One puts his hand on one knee and the other sitting on the left side of her puts his hand on her other knee. " I can really use a good time with 2 men." She leans over and kisses one then leans the other way and kiss the other and says "lets get the fuck outta here and you both give it to me.

They check into a cheap motel 3 blocks over and go crazy for hours. When they were done she said " you both want a $10,000 a month allowance and be my boy toys? If you want this I'm going to need your help but you will never have to work again, how does that sound?"

CHAPTER 5

The Next Surgery

Talking with her husband, she gets in a one on one intimate conversation and he is still down because his lover left him she could tell. Though she is not supposed to know about it.

Kim- "I know you've been talking about surgery especially for a bigger penis and the wrinkles in your face. I am ready to accept that and will be in charge of it if you want, so no one at the facility will know what surgery you're getting."

Doug: "That's great, it's for you I'm doing it for."

Kim: "I know and I will probably really enjoy it. I already told my parents to watch the kids all next week so we can recover and test drive your new appendage. We will do it this weekend and give all the weekend workers off with pay so we are alone."

Doug: " That's a fuckin great plan, I love you so much."

Kim: " Let's figure this out,

So Saturday comes around, it's 4 a.m., he's naked on the table and strapped down. Kim has him right where she wants him and brought in a little plastic box with her. He is injected and while getting tired she moves a tray over him.

Doug: " Honey what are you doing?"

Kim: " After what you put me through, I took care of Debbie and it's time to take care of you." She picks up a giant serrated knife and says " watch this." Then takes the knife to the base of his penis and cuts it slowly off as he screams. She sets it on the tray above him and dices it up and feeds it to a couple of rats she brought in the box. Blood is coming out of what's left and she puts gauze in there to halt the bleeding then starts the robotic arms up and he finally passes out. Ever since she flew back she has been in close contact with the parolees who were waiting to be called to the facility. They had to wait because with all the security cameras he might have noticed them coming in. A vagina is being constructed and at the same time getting g size breasts. But since the chest is already open, recently an 80 year old man had all 4 heart valves replaced, those 80 year old heart valves are now being put into her husband. The really big 3d printed breasts are now coming down the conveyor belt as his legs are opened wide to have the vagina formed. The parolees are watching as she kisses one then the other. "You both can live with me, I've wanted this and now you two men can be my kids daddy's, I will make sure the kids call you both dad.

Also I will legally change their last names too. One will have your last name and the other will have yours" as she points to the other guy. "I am going to eliminate him entirely from myself and the kids' lives."

Doug wakes up with the sun beating down on him. He plants his hands down to try and sit up and realizes he's naked on some beach. When he gets coherent and leans up the breasts are swinging, hitting his stomach and pulling on him. He looks down and is shocked, "what the fuck? Oh

god, that fuckin bitch, what happened got damn it." From the sun hitting on them and no meds they are bloated, sunburned, swollen, and oozing along the stitch lines. He stands up but staggers and sees his vagina, puts his hand down there and screams " she removed my fuckin dick!" Then cries. She starts walking but having trouble getting her balance with all that new extra weight. Her vagina is swollen as well and in severe pain from infection because of the sand and heat and tries to walk faster hoping to come across some village or a bar or shop or a person. She can't catch her breath and has to stop every 8-10 steps and gets really weak not knowing that 80 year old heart valves were put in. Doug finally realizes where she is at, on the island she purchased with no food or water and remembers warning all the other islands to make sure those residents stay at least 10 miles away. After walking about 15 minutes more falls to her knees, the stress on her heart is too much and has to lay and rest.

1 month later, Kim, now pregnant and her 2 lovers come back by boat to the island and see no signs of Doug. They walk around a little, then think they see her near some rocks next to the beach. She is laying there on her back, the breasts now 3 times the size of the implants. They walk up to her and the breasts are moving. As they lean down, 3 rats appear out of a small hole they made in the breasts and run towards the trees. Her mouth is partially open and roaches with their eggs are in there. Looking down, maggots are so packed in the vagina area and it's so swollen, you can't see any detail of it anymore. They all left after seeing that fully satisfied and not grossed out at all.

CHAPTER 6

The Bayou

2 years later, Kim comes for a visit. A 2 year old beautiful baby is in a crib at Buck's home.

Kim: " She is so beautiful. Are you taking good care of the mom? Now the cousins can grow up together, it's nice to have cousins around the same age."

Buck: " Oh yes, she gets hers now that I have my daughter. I named her debrina. Yep they can have a nice close relationship."

Kim: " No ones found the car?"

Buck: " nope"

Kim's daughter comes up to her- " Mom, for a school project I want to be black for 3 months, can I do that?"

Kim: " Sure, I will get the code together and change you next week" If you would like you can go longer, I can change you back at any time. After it's done we will go online and legally change your name and identity and nationality and get a completely new ID for you. We will also put down the time limit for when you want the state of CA. to flip everything back, It only takes a few minutes on their website. I did 4 girls in the past couple of months. One wanted to be Asian, A black girl wanted to be white, another caucasian girl wanted to be Indonesian and the Asian girl wanted to be from India. Now go over there and think of a good first and last name for your new identity."

She then picks up Debrina and looks out the window. Debbie is in her enclosure with both ankles cuffed on each side of the bar making her legs spread wide open . Buck has her in that position for 2 hours a day and one of the mastiffs is allowed in there each day to do what male dogs in heat always do. Kim walks outside and looks close up at her face and sees red bumps all over it and black spots that seem to be moving. " Oh you poor thing," she says to Debbie, realizing those red bumps are small bites and those black spots are ticks and fleas crawling all over her face.

End

Printed in the USA
CPSIA information can be obtained
at www.ICGtesting.com
LVHW010739210923
758625LV00005B/80